TITANIC TIMES

A Diary
For April 1912

Allison   Murphy

Belcouver Press
1997

First published 1997 by
Belcouver Press
Box 117
1857 West 4th Avenue
Vancouver B.C.
V6J 1M4
Canada

Reprinted 2000 by
Belfast Swiftprint Limited

Reprinted 2012 by
Dorman & Sons Limited

Canadian Cataloguing in Publication Data
Murphy, Allison, 1948-
Titanic Times

ISBN 0-9699464-2-2
1. Titanic (Steamship) — Fiction I. Title.
PR6063.U727T5 1997   8823'.914   C97-910274-X

Printed by
Dorman & Sons Limited
Unit 2, 2A Apollo Road, Belfast BT12 6HP
Tel: (028) 9266 6700 · Fax: (028) 9266 1881

FOREWORD

This wonderful fictional diary of James McDermott, growing up in the shadow of the massive gantries of Harland & Wolff in Belfast, is based totally on fact. Through the eyes of a twelve year old boy, the reader is taken back in time to see the city that built *Titanic*. The ordinary everyday activities mentioned give a fascinating insight into society at the time and the facts have been meticulously researched. When James writes that the balloon ascent and parachute descent planned for Easter Monday, 8th April 1912, were cancelled due to the weather, that's exactly what happened. We learn about his interests and the lives his family lead, as well as the impact the news of the sinking of *Titanic* had on them all. James's scrapbook provides a fascinating overview of newspaper coverage at the time.

This little book sets *Titanic* firmly in the correct context. It will appeal to all ages and James becomes a friend. Allison Murphy, who has based the book on the memories of those who were alive in 1912- Norman Douglas, Ena McKenna, Johnny Marquis, Annie Stewart, Mary Thompson, John Parkinson- opens up a portal in time which invites us back to see the people who built *Titanic* ... in their own back yards.

Allison has studied this period of history and her teaching background allows her excellent communication skills to bring the city which built *Titanic* to life. "Titanic Times" is a book not to be missed, to be enjoyed by all ... granny to grandchild as well as those solely interested in the *Titanic* story... a gem of a book with widespread appeal.

Una Reilly MBE
Belfast Titanic Society, Chairman and Co-Founder
Belfast 2012

1912

January

S	M	T	W	T	F	S
	1	2	3	4	5	6
7	8	9	10	11	12	13
14	15	16	17	18	19	20
21	22	23	24	25	26	27
28	29	30	31			

February

S	M	T	W	T	F	S
				1	2	3
4	5	6	7	8	9	10
11	12	13	14	15	16	17
18	19	20	21	22	23	24
25	26	27	28	29		

March

S	M	T	W	T	F	S
					1	2
3	4	5	6	7	8	9
10	11	12	13	14	15	16
17	18	19	20	21	22	23
24	25	26	27	28	29	30
31						

April

S	M	T	W	T	F	S
	1	2	3	4	5	6
7	8	9	10	11	12	13
14	15	16	17	18	19	20
21	22	23	24	25	26	27
28	29	30				

May

S	M	T	W	T	F	S
			1	2	3	4
5	6	7	8	9	10	11
12	13	14	15	16	17	18
19	20	21	22	23	24	25
26	27	28	29	30	31	

June

S	M	T	W	T	F	S
						1
2	3	4	5	6	7	8
9	10	11	12	13	14	15
16	17	18	19	20	21	22
23	24	25	26	27	28	29
30						

July

S	M	T	W	T	F	S
	1	2	3	4	5	6
7	8	9	10	11	12	13
14	15	16	17	18	19	20
21	22	23	24	25	26	27
28	29	30	31			

August

S	M	T	W	T	F	S
				1	2	3
4	5	6	7	8	9	10
11	12	13	14	15	16	17
18	19	20	21	22	23	24
25	26	27	28	29	30	31

September

S	M	T	W	T	F	S
1	2	3	4	5	6	7
8	9	10	11	12	13	14
15	16	17	18	19	20	21
22	23	24	25	26	27	28
29	30					

October

S	M	T	W	T	F	S
		1	2	3	4	5
6	7	8	9	10	11	12
13	14	15	16	17	18	19
20	21	22	23	24	25	26
27	28	29	30	31		

November

S	M	T	W	T	F	S
					1	2
3	4	5	6	7	8	9
10	11	12	13	14	15	16
17	18	19	20	21	22	23
24	25	26	27	28	29	30

December

S	M	T	W	T	F	S
1	2	3	4	5	6	7
8	9	10	11	12	13	14
15	16	17	18	19	20	21
22	23	24	25	26	27	28
29	30	31				

April 1912

Sun	Mon	Tue	Wed	Thu	Fri	Sat
My birthday. Full moon.	**1** Distillery v Belfast Blues	**2** See Titanic leave Belfast	**3** Uncle Thomas visits.	**4** Went to my granny's.	**5** At the park.	**6** Matinee
7 Easter Sunday	**8** Rolled our eggs. WET!	**9** No school.	**10** On the tramcar.	**11** Titanic left South-hampton.	**12** Caught smicks.	**13** Bath night
14 On train to Newtownards	**15** Titanic in collision	**16** Titanic has sunk!!	**17** School - sad.	**18** Start scrapbook	**19** Uncle Thomas for tea	**20** Matinee - The Cow Boy Pugilist
21 At my granny's	**22** Mother got a new coat	**23** Learnt poem	**24** School inspection	**25** Letter from America	**26** Saw the New York Times	**27** In trouble
28 A day in town	**29** Mary sick.	**30** Took my scrapbook in to school.				

It was my twelfth birthday yesterday and I still have the shiny sixpence that my father gave me. I was born on the thirty-first day of March in the year 1900 in Belfast, Ireland. When I told my teacher, Mr.Cunningham, about my birthday he pointed at all the Kings and Queens who are up on the wall of the schoolroom and said,

'James McDermott, you have already lived through three of those Kings and Queens. Queen Victoria was on the throne when you were born, then came her son Edward VII and now his son, George V is the King.'

I told my mother that when I came home for lunch but she was too busy ladling the soup out to answer me. She had been washing all morning and the house smelt of soap. All the clothes were on the line in the yard and my mother kept watching out of the scullery window in case the rain came on. Her hands were red from all the scrubbing and the kings and queens meant little to her.

I asked could I use my money and go to see the football match at Grosvenor Park tonight. Distillery is my favourite team and they were playing the Belfast Blues. My mother clipped my ear and said there were better ways to spend sixpence and in any case my father wouldn't be home from work until after seven o'clock.

There seemed to be thousands and thousands of people on the shores of Belfast Lough today, all to watch the biggest ship in the world sail away to Southampton. The great occasion was a general holiday because the ship had been built right here by Harland and Wolff. My father took Tommy and me all the way to Greencastle on the tramcar to watch it. We were so excited that father was constantly telling us to sit or stand at peace.

After waiting for what seemed like hours we heard the sirens sounding and saw the great Titanic heading up Belfast Lough. To me the ship looked nearly as big as the lough itself. Smoke belched from three of her four funnels and we could imagine the engineers feverishly stoking the boilers to get up steam. The great ship was being pulled up the lough by about a dozen tugboats. Father said that some of the tugs had come specially from Liverpool to assist the White Star liner. We could make out the names on a few of them, Herculaneum, Haskisson, Herald and Wallasey.

When the ship reached the mouth of Belfast Lough we heard the great noise of the enormous propeller blades and saw the sea being churned up. The Titanic was off across the sea and everyone cheered. Men threw their caps in the air and we waved our hankies. I felt a wee bit sad.

Wednesday 3rd April 1912

All day in school we talked about the Titanic and the sight we had seen yesterday. Joseph Barrett talked so much that he had to stand in the corner.

After dinner Uncle Thomas came to our house and I sat on the stairs and listened while he talked to my father. Uncle Thomas works in the shipyard and my mother says that he talks so much about the Titanic you would think he had built it all by himself. Tonight he could talk about nothing else, he said he felt so proud to watch her leave yesterday.

'Did you know, James,' he said to my father, 'there are eight steel decks amidships and an extra deck at each end? Can you imagine what three million rivets look like, that's what we put in her? The ones we put in the hull plate were an inch and a half in diameter. And the rudder, what a rudder, it was that big we had to cast it in six pieces. It's as big as a house. The whole ship is nearly nine hundred feet long and as tall as a building with eleven stories. Can you believe it? The public rooms are a marvel to see, the Jacobean dining saloon has rose carpet and there's even leaded glass in one of the lounges. There's a gymnasium and a squash racquet court, Turkish baths and a real swimming pool. On board a ship! Did you ever hear the like of that, James?'

I think my mother was glad when he had his cup of tea and went home but I could have listened all night.

We studied Geography in school today. Mr. Cunningham rolled down the big map on the wall that has the whole wide world stretched out flat. He used the long wooden pointer to show us the route of the Titanic which is in Southampton now.

After getting all the provisions and some passengers on board the ship will travel to Cherbourg in France. The last passenger stop before going to New York will be in Queenstown in Cork. We had to write it all down in our books and then add up how many miles the ship would travel between leaving Belfast and arriving in the port of New York. It looked like this:

Belfast, Ireland to Southampton, England	471
Southampton to Cherbourg, France	84
Cherbourg to Queenstown, Ireland	307
Queenstown to New York, America	2825
Total -	3687 miles

After school I took some soda farls that my mother had baked up to my granny's house. I told her how far the Titanic would travel and she said that to her that seemed a very long way to go for she had never been more than ten miles from a cow's tail.

My granny and granda never forget to remind us that they came up to Belfast all the way from County Tyrone.

Friday 5th April 1912

It was very warm and sunny today and Tommy and I went to the park with Bertie and Hugh. We played churchie and marlies and had a game of football with a ball that Bertie had made from some old clothes. Bertie wanted to know if we would have enough money to go to the matinee tomorrow because he had heard that the picture on at the Alhambra, 'The Girl and the Motor Boat' was really good. I have my sixpence and tuppence of that would pay for Tommy and me if we're allowed.

From the park we could see some people with luggage waiting for the tramcar. Hugh said that they were lucky and must be going away for Easter now that the weather was so good. His mother had wanted to go away but his father had said that it cost as much as thirty-eight shillings to go away to a hotel for Easter and the most they would be doing was a day excursion to Portrush at four shillings and sixpence. That sounds like a lot of money to me.

Bertie said that the only place he would like to go to was Dublin. He had read in his father's paper that Buffalo Bill's Wild West Show was coming to the Jones' Road Grounds in Dublin this month and the real William Cody would be there. There would be eight hundred cowboys and cowgirls, four hundred Indians and two thousand horses. We all agreed that that would be a real excursion.

Saturday 6th April 1912

We are not allowed to go anywhere near the pawnshop, my mother says that it is not the sort of place we should be in or about, but today Bertie, Tommy and I walked past on our way home from the matinee. I did not have to pay for Tommy because Uncle Thomas came to our house last night and gave us a penny each for Easter. Hugh couldn't come with us because his family had gone to the point to point races at Ballyhaft near Newtownards.

There was a wee girl from a standard below me in school just standing outside the pawnshop with a big parcel wrapped in newspaper under her arm. As we got closer we shouted to her but she turned away as if she didn't recognise us. We stopped and didn't know what to do. As we watched an old woman came by and the girl said, ' Missis, are you going in, can I go in with you?' The woman took the girl in with her and Bertie wanted us to go close to the window and look in and see what happened in there. I was afraid my father might pass by and see us so I ran away.

I told my mother when we got home and she said the wee girl's father must be out of work and the family had to pawn his clothes to buy food. I can't help wondering how he will ever be able to work if he has no clothes or boots.

Mother boiled eggs for us this morning and left them to cool in the meat safe in the yard while we were all at church. When we came home we weren't allowed to get them out until after we had had our dinner. I ate my potatoes, bacon and cabbage as fast as I could and then got out the old newspapers from the glory hole under the stairs.

After the table had been cleared I spread out the papers on it and brought the eggs in from the yard. My sisters, Mary and Eileen, could hardly wait as my father boiled up the water and then Tommy and I dissolved the yellow dolly dye in my mother's big brown baking bowl. When it was ready we all put our eggs in and Father said that since the sun was shining we would all go out for a walk while the colour set. We had taken off our Sunday clothes to dye the eggs and Mother said we had to put them all on again. Tommy moaned that he didn't know why we couldn't just wear our old corduroys but Mother said we daren't go out on a Sunday in our weekday clothes. She helped Mary and Eileen while Father wrapped the stale bread in some newspaper.

It was like a summer's day as we walked along beside the Lagan and I thought of all the lucky people at the seaside for the Easter holidays. Then we came upon a family of swans and I forgot the seaside as they ambled up to us to take our bread. When we got home again our eggs were as yellow as the sun.

My mother and
father in
their best
clothes

Monday 8th April 1912

When we woke up this morning we heard heavy rain beating against the window. Tommy and I got dressed under the blankets and rushed downstairs for our porridge. We were heart scared that we would have to stay in but Mother said we would still go to roll our eggs. We must wrap up well because it was very windy.

Between the heavy showers we all made our way to the park where lots of other children had gathered to roll their eggs down the dummy hill. By the time my egg reached the bottom it was smashed into smithereens but I ate it anyway. Bertie was there and he made us all keep watching the sky because he said there was going to be a grand balloon ascent and parachute descent. All we could see were grey clouds and when there was another heavy shower Mother made us go home before we were soaked through.

My granny and granda came for their tea tonight and we had lovely slices of ham. My granny said a man on the tramcar told her they'd had to cancel the balloon ascent because of the weather. It was the wildest and wettest Easter Monday anyone could remember. After tea Mother and Father went to see a Kinemacolour picture at the Grand Opera House and my granda lit the lamps and told us stories about a great white stallion. We watched the lamplighter go past with his long pole and light the street lamps. I am sure he was soaked to the skin.

My mother bought
this polish because
she read about it
in the newspaper.
I used it today
on the brass rods
from the stairs
but it didn't make
the job any easier.

MONKEY BRAND.

When the Gong sounds for Meals

YOU will sit down to the table with a better relish for the meal if you know that Monkey Brand is used freely in the kitchen. Monkey Brand means bright, wholesome cleanliness—but cleanliness without drudgery. Monkey Brand works quickly, easily and thoroughly. It should have a place in every household.

WON'T WASH CLOTHES.
2 BARS FOR 4D.

Makes Copper like Gold—Tin like Silver—Paint like new.

BENJAMIN BROOKE & COMPANY LIMITED.

M 12??–14

We had to help Mother before we went out to play today. Tommy had to bring in the coal and then clean the hearth and the brass fender. I had to take all the brass rods off the lino on the stairs and bring them down to the kitchen and polish them. It is the chore I hate most. Even Mary had to help and dust the hallstand and shelves. She wasn't allowed to dust in the parlour in case she broke any of the good ornaments kept in there.

For our lunch Mother beat an egg up in the potatoes. We put butter in the middle and tried to stop it escaping as it melted. Bertie came to our house in the afternoon. He said that his father, a tramcar driver, was off work for the day. The Lord Mayor of Belfast, a man called Robert J. McMordie, has closed all the roads because there is some big procession to the Balmoral Showgrounds. Bertie's father had told him that one hundred thousand men would be going to Balmoral and his tramcar would not have been able to travel along the lines. My mother said that it is all because some people want something called Home Rule and others do not. She said it was nothing to do with us and we would be better off going outside with our marbles instead of harrishing her off the face of the earth.

She added that she was glad Father had to go to his work because putting food on the table was far more important for people like us.

I went to the tramcar teminus today with Bertie. The terminus is at the end of our street and Bertie takes his father's tea down to him when he is working. We took a can of tea and some sandwiches wrapped up in a cloth and watched as the double-ended tramcar swung round, hauling its electrical trolley rope with it.

Mr. Nulty was waiting for us with his greatcoat pulled up to his ears. It was a cool day and he had no windows to protect him from wind and rain. When he saw us he said, 'Lads, do you want to come on board?' We leapt on board because sometimes he let us go upstairs to change the seat-backs round. We can see all the way down the road from the open-topped deck.

Today, for the first time, he brought us to stand beside him and we could see all the wonders of his tramcar. The sand pin where he released sand with his right foot onto icy tram lines. The gong at his left foot which he rang to let people know the tramcar was coming. The huge handbrake which he used to stop it and the cog that he kicked into place with his great boot. And then, the most special thing of all. He let us turn the canopies and we changed the destinations round. As the numbers moved I could imagine the tramcar travelling to distant places which we had now labelled it with.

CLIFTONVILLE, OLDPARK, SPRINGFIELD, MALONE.

Thursday 11th April 1912

Bertie's new sister came today. We were playing kick-the-tin outside and we saw the nurse come down the street swinging her black bag. Bertie said that the new baby must be in the bag and would cost five shillings. He had heard his mother tell his father that she did not know how many five shillings she could find. Bertie already has three brothers and two sisters. His brothers were playing with an old bit of rope in the road and my mother told Bertie to go and bring them up to our house and she would make us all champ for dinner. She boiled up extra potatoes and made potato bread which she took down to Bertie's house. Bertie wasn't happy about another sister.

After dinner my father played 'mountain, river,lake' with us because it was too wet to go out. Father picked a letter from the newspaper and we all had to name a mountain or a river or whatever that started with it. Bertie's smallest brother is still in petticoats so he couldn't play and started to cry. Father made Mary and Eileen get out all the bits of delph they had collected and play with him. I think my father was glad when Bertie's father came from work and took them all home.

Father read out that the Titanic left Southampton yesterday and was described in the newspaper as 'the newest ocean giant'. I'm so proud she was built here in Belfast in the biggest shipyard in the world.

Friday 12th April 1912

A man died down our street last night and all the blinds in the houses round about were closed this morning. My mother said that he had been in Whiteabbey with tuberculosis and he had already lost two sons to the same thing. She said when the disease got into a house it could carry off a whole family. All day she was cleaning the house, scrubbing the floors, windows and doors. When Tommy and I walked up to call for Bertie all the women seemed to be doing the same thing. Some women were beating mats out the front and others had all their bedclothes out on the lines in their yards.

Bertie, Tommy and I walked on round to Hugh's house which has a wee garden out the front. His father has a gramophone and Hugh said he would let us see it. When we got there Hugh's mother wouldn't let him bring us in. She said a gramophone record costs half a crown and we might break it. Maybe they haven't as much money as Hugh lets on.

We all decided to go down to the river and look for smicks instead. Hugh brought a jamjar and we took off our shoes and socks and paddled in the water. It came right up over the bottom of our trousers to our knees. That was more fun anyway.

When we walked home there were lots of men standing on the corner. They were talking about some bill that had been passed in parliament but they lowered their voices as we passed by.

Saturday 13th April 1912

Tommy and I had to stay upstairs tonight because Mary and Eileen were having their baths. Beforehand I had to carry the big bath in from its nail in the yard and Tommy had to put extra coal on the fire. I set the bath in front of the hearth and Mother came in and out with pots full of hot water. After she had filled the bath she moved two chairs behind it and hung a blanket over them so my little sisters would not get a draught. My mother was always afraid of them catching the cold or something worse. She brought them in from the front step where they had been playing houses and sent Tommy and me away with a, 'Don't come back until you are called'.

We played tents in the bedroom and we camped in the middle of a desert surrounded by fierce Arabs. We were in great danger and had to use our shoes as swords to fend off attack. Then we made our bed a sailing ship and went in search of riches to the South Pacific Ocean. Strange savages kept attacking us there too. We must have made a lot of noise because Mother came up with the wet flannel in her hand and both of us yelled at the sting on our thighs. She made us tidy up all the blankets before we came down for our own baths.

By the time we got downstairs the water in the tin bath was nearly cold and Mother said we had nobody to blame but ourselves. Tommy and I had the fastest bath ever!

My wee sisters, Mary and Eileen, in their Christmas photograph.

Sunday 14th April 1912

My other granny, my father's mother, lives near Newtownards and my mother said that it was time we went to visit her. That meant that we had to get up really early this morning and put on our Sunday clothes. Luckily we didn't need to get washed. We got a tramcar down to Station Street where the County Down Railway has its station. The return tickets cost a shilling each which is why we can't go and see my granny very often.

I love to sit on the train and look out as it passes through town and country. There are five stops on the way at Bloomfield, Neill's Hill, Knock, Dundonald and Comber. By the time we reached Comber station almost every seat was taken. At Newtownards everyone got off and we had to walk over a mile to my granny's house. On the way a bus passed us, it had no top and hard tyres and Father said it was as comfortable to walk as use that bus. My granny was all smiles to see us and gave us steaming bowls of soup with floury potatoes in the middle. My granny grows all her own vegetables and makes sure we eat lots of them when we visit. She is sure that there is no fresh food in a big city like Belfast. Afterwards Tommy and I took Mary and Eileen to pick the last of the daffodils which grow wild in the fields behind my granny's.

The walk back to the train made Eileen cry and Father had to carry her. We were all exhausted by the time we got home.

Monday 15th April 1912

School started again this morning and Tommy and I had to trail Mary along because she did not want to go. She is always afraid that she will be caned. If your work is bad in our school you are made to stand in the corner. Every half an hour the headmaster walks round and anyone found in the corner is caned. I told Mary to do her work well and she would not be put in the corner but she said that her writing in her copybook is not good and she cannot get it any better.

I did not see her again until after school and by then I was more worried about something I had heard one of the masters say. He said that the Titanic had been in a collison.

My father brought the Belfast Telegraph home with him tonight and we all sat down to read it. The headlines said:

<u>THE TITANIC SINKING</u>

<u>NO DANGER OF LOSS OF LIFE</u>

<u>ICEBERG 70 MILES IN LENGTH</u>

The paper reported that the Titanic had been in a collison with an iceberg off the coast of Newfoundland and was sinking. Uncle Thomas came round to our house to see if we had a newspaper. He read the headlines with a frown on his face and then announced that she would never sink and Captain Smith would bring her back to Belfast for repairs. My uncle says that she is built in such a way that even with water in her she will float.

Everyone in school was very quiet today. As we walked home all the women were outside their doors talking to each other and shaking their heads. My mother said that everyone was sad because the Titanic really had sunk. I can not believe that that wonderful ship I watched leaving Belfast just two weeks ago is now at the bottom of the Atlantic Ocean. Men said she was unsinkable and that day in Belfast Lough she looked so big that I thought nothing could ever harm her.

Uncle Thomas came straight to our house after work and he just sat at the table and held his head in his hands. He was crying. I have never seen a man cry before. He had just heard that not only has the Titanic sunk but fifteen hundred people have gone down with her. It seems that some of his friends from the shipyard were on board and are lost. He said even Mr. Andrews, the managing director of Harland and Wolff, was thought to have perished.

Uncle Thomas thought the world of Mr. Andrews because they had entered service in the same year, 1899, and Mr. Andrews had worked as long hours as everyone else. Only the other day Uncle Thomas had boasted about knowing the boss so well and about all the millionaires that were aboard the ship he had helped to build.

He was so proud of that ship and tonight he looked as though his heart was breaking.

Wednesday 17th April 1912

Everyone in school was talking about the Titanic today and no one really seemed to believe what had happened. Mr. Cunningham said that he'd heard she was going too fast. For so long that great ship seemed to rise up over all the buildings in Belfast and now she is at the very bottom of the sea.

I keep remembering a Sunday when Uncle Thomas took Tommy and me out for the day. Our uncle is a great bird-watcher and on his Sundays off he sometimes takes us to the fourteen mile long Belfast Lough and points out the wigeon, golden-eye ducks and geese which come here in Winter.

One Sunday, some months ago, Uncle Thomas took us on a tramcar to Harland and Wolff shipyard at the Queen's Island where the great ship, Titanic, lay in the Thompson Graving dry dock. He told us that gallons of paint to prevent rust had been applied by an army of painters in white overalls. Tommy and I stood in awe to think that our uncle had helped build this huge ship. We felt like little insects as we gazed upwards.

I know it was naughty of me but I cut off a splinter of woodwork from the gangway as a memento and I have kept it in a matchbox ever since. I never thought then that a few months later there would be nothing of that wondeful ship left.

Now I will keep that tiny piece of wood for ever and ever.

Everyone was so busy talking about the Titanic last night that mother forgot to make the porridge. I was not sorry because she let us have sugar sandwiches for breakfast. I would like to make a scrapbook about the Titanic so I asked could I have the newspapers when I came home from school. I cut out the headlines first.

LOSS OF THE TITANIC

DEATH TOLL 1,490

Disastrous End To Maiden Voyage

THE KING'S MESSAGE TO THE PRESIDENT

THE PRESIDENT'S MESSAGE TO THE KING

FURTHER HOPE ABANDONED

Gloom in the City of the Leviathan's Birth

Of course Mr. Thomas Andrews was written about but so too were the officers and some of the men Uncle Thomas knew. *Many of the officers, engineering staff and crew are natives of Ireland, not a few hailing from Belfast and the North. The chief medical officer is Dr. O'Loughlin who belongs to the South of Ireland and his assistant is Dr.John Simpson. Amongst the engineering staff is Mr.H.G.Harvey of Belfast. One of the plumbers is Mr.Frank Parkes, Belfast. Mr.Anthony Frost, of Bloomfield, a leading hand at Messrs. Harland & Wolff's, was also on board. It is stated that another Belfast man on board the Titanic was Mr.Bertie Irvine, an electrician, who is a son of Mr.Irvine, rate collector, of Merryfield.*

Uncle Thomas came for his tea tonight. Mother made his favourite, boiled sausages and onions. She thought it might cheer him up but one of the accounts I had cut out of the newspaper made him bring out his big grey handkerchief again.

The Titanic in Belfast

For months past her giant hull and towering funnels constituted a local spectacle as she lay at the fitting-out wharf - a symbol of the power and force enshrined in the great shipyard out of which she had emerged. She was pointed out to visitors as one of our principal sights for the time being, and her huge bulk was first to catch the eye of the rambler around the high-lying environs of Belfast when he paused to survey the panorama of the city, country and scene visible from the hills. She was, in a sense, a part of Belfast, and the spectators who watched her steaming down the lough a couple of weeks ago, magnificently representative of the Northern capital's engineering enterprise, felt a subtle regret at the removal of such an imposing product of the city from the harbour mouth.

Uncle Thomas said he wished she were still in Belfast instead of two miles down on the bed of the North Atlantic.

The newspapers say that over fourteen hundred people are dead. Father has reckoned that that is four times the number of men, women and children who live in our street.

Saturday 20th April 1912

Bertie and Hugh called for Tommy and me this morning to see if we could go to the park. Mother told us to run on. I think she was glad to get us out. Uncle Thomas was round again because the shipyard was closed as a sign of respect for all the people who died. Mother says she can get nothing done with all the hullaballoo and she feels like the wreck of the Hesperus.

There were a lot of other children in the park, all chased out to enjoy the sunny day. We played football with some boys from the next street and some of us pretended we were the Irish team that beat Wales three to two last Saturday. We started fighting because one of the boys wouldn't let us score our third goal. Hugh said he had to go home because his father was taking him to a dogshow. They have a Kerry Blue which is very fierce but his father thinks there is no other dog like it and he is always plucking it and fixing its beard. When we go to his house we are always warned never to go into the yard in case the dog is out. Hugh took his ball with him so we had to stop the game anyway.

In the afternoon Father gave us tuppence to go to the matinee. The Cow Boy Pugilist was on and a boy beside me gave me three boiled sweets to read it to him. I sucked them all the way home and Tommy complained that I was dilly-dallying so that Father wouldn't know I'd taken the sweets.

Sunday 21st April 1912

    Last night I had to polish all our boots for church this morning and we all set off in our Sunday best. After church we walked up the road to granny's for our dinner. Even though it is only a mile Father had to carry Eileen on his shoulders when she cried. By the time we got there Mother's best dress was all dusty along the bottom and our boots looked as though I had never used all that Cherry Blossom on them. Tommy and I sat with my granda while he filled and smoked his pipe. We love to hear him talk about when he was a wee boy like us.

'We didn't have all these new-fangled contraptions you see nowadays, ships like hotels, motorised vehicles and even machines that can carry a man up in the sky. When I was a lad and came here from Tyrone there was only a quarter of these people in Belfast and no fancy City Hall either. Most people lived out in the country with only a few potatoes to eat and maybe a bit of fish. They knew how to work too, no fancy schools for big boys like you. At your age I was doing a man's job and your granny was a half-timer, going to school for half the day and working on the wet mill floor the other half. You boys don't know you're living, school all day and running water inside your house. I had to walk half a mile to get water then. I remember my mother telling me that during the famine they had to skin rats to eat.'

I didn't really enjoy my granny's dinner today.

Uncle   Thomas
with Mary
and our
cousin Rose.

Sports Coats

THE vogue of the Sports Coat is as popular as ever, and we have met the demand with a splendid collection of every weave and every style that is most wanted.

My mother's new coat was in the newspaper today. It looks much better on Mother.

Monday 22nd April 1912

Eileen cried when we all left for school this morning. She would like to go to school but she is too young so she has to stay at home. Mother tried to cheer her up by telling her that they were going into town and she could wear the new bonnet she got for Easter But even the new bonnet and the promised tramcar ride did not stop her crying. Mother gave us some bread and jam to take to school because she would not be at home and she wrote our names on the paper she wrapped it in. At school we put our pieces in the big basket at the front and the teacher gave them out to us when twelve o'clock came.

We had some time to play in the schoolyard afterwards and I lost one of my best marlies to Jimmy Scott. He called me funkyknuckle because I didn't bulk the marlie straight and we wrestled on the ground. Then he said he would give it back to me if I gave him a cigarette but I told him I couldn't because I didn't have any. They cost thruppence for ten and anyway I don't like the taste.

Eileen was happy again by the time we all got home and so was Mother. She had bought a new coat and she was so pleased because she had been putting the money away for a long time and when she got to Newell's the coat had money off. She put the coat on and walked about the house like a toff. That made us all laugh.

We did handwriting in school today. I had to do it twice because I made a big blot just before I finished my first copy. Then the teacher said we had to learn it by heart because we are in the season of Spring. Now I can write it without looking at my book.

A primrose awoke from its long winter sleep
And stretched out its head through its green leaves to peep.
But the air was so cold and the wind was so keen,
Not a bright flower but itself could be seen.
Alas, said the primrose, no use to deny
Here all alone half hidden I lie.
I'll try to be cheerful, contented to be
Just a simple wild flower growing under a tree.
Soon a maiden passed by looking weary and sad,
In the bright Irish springtime when all should be glad.
She saw the primrose so bright and so gay,
And decided it charmed all her sadness away.
The primrose gave thanks to the dear Lord above
Who had sent along such a submission of love.

When I recited it to my mother she said she thought it was a lovely poem and I said it so well I should enter one of those verse-speaking competitions. I'd be a laughing stock.

Wednesday 24th April 1912

The national inspector made his annual visit to our school today and I was very embarrassed when I was brought out to answer his questions. He asked me what did I know about Ireland so I recited what I had been taught from the Longman's Shilling Geography:

Ireland is the second island in point of size of the British islands and lies to the west of Great Britain. Ireland is divided into four great provinces, they are Ulster, Leinster, Munster and Connacht.

Then he asked what did I know about Ulster and again I recited:

The main town of Ulster is Belfast on Belfast Lough. It has two hundred thousand inhabitants and the industries are cotton and linen manufacturing, distilling, shipping and shipbuilding. Ulster contains the world's largest shipyard, ropeworks, tobacco factory, linen-spinning mill, tea machinery works and aereated water factory.

The Inspector seemed pleased and told me to sit down. After school some of the other boys punched me and laughed at me for being a show-off and I ran home crying. I was only doing what I was asked. The teacher wants me to sit a big exam for a scholarship now that I am through my books but after today I don't want to.

Thursday 25th April 1912

A letter came to our house this morning and I heard the postman say to mother 'that'll be from your Rose'. Rose is my mother's sister and she went to America to live when I was a wee boy in petticoats. All I can remember is a pretty lady with lots of auburn hair and my mother crying a lot when she waved her off at the boat. I think she was very brave to go to a country she had never seen but her letters always make Mother cry, she says that Rose is very homesick. Aunt Rose lives in a big city called Boston and is in service there. That sounds very grand to me but my granny says she's just a glorified scullery-maid and would never have gone if her head hadn't been turned by stories which her friend told her. I don't think my granny has ever forgiven her for going.

This particular letter did not make Mother cry, instead she had her hat and coat on when I left for school. She was going up to my granny's to tell her the news. Aunt Rose has found a man and was married on St.Patrick's day just past.

Mother let me read the letter when I came home from school and Aunt Rose seemed very happy. This man has a farm and two hundred acres of his own and she has gone to live far outside Boston.

I asked was my granny pleased but my mother just shook her head. I think two hundred acres should please anybody.

Father and Mother have gone to the Panopticon tonight and my Uncle Thomas is minding us. They are going to see 'The Mermaid' and 'The Stolen Violin'. Uncle Thomas said they didn't sound like pictures Father would enjoy but Father said that Mother didn't know that the English Cup Final was on as well so he would be seeing Barnsley play West Bromich. Uncle Thomas laughed at that. It is the first time I have seen him laugh since the Titanic sank.

Mother told him about Aunt Rose and said it was a pity he couldn't find a good woman to marry. He said that good women were few and far between and anyway he would never find one as handsome as my mother in her new coat. That made them all laugh.

When he had put Mary and Eileen to bed and listened to their prayers Uncle Thomas took out a newspaper which someone had brought into work and he showed it to Tommy and me. It was the New York Times. It was dated Tuesday, April 16th 1912 and cost one cent. The front page told all about the sinking of the Titanic and had two big pictures, one of the Titanic leaving Belfast and one of Captain Smith. I asked Uncle Thomas could I have the newspaper for my scrapbook but he said no because he only had a lend of it. He said I could copy out the bits I wanted. I never saw a newspaper from America before.

My mother was cross with me today even though it was not really my fault. She sent me down to the wee shop in a house down our street. It sells sweets, matches, dummy tits, paraffin and camphorated oil and some groceries. We don't get our messages there but mother had run out of sugar and needed it quickly. She was baking because Uncle John, Aunt Ruby and my cousin Rose were coming for tea to hear all about Aunt Rose and the man she has married. My mother says Aunt Ruby is very nosy and we are to be sure we don't let her know any of our business. Mother's arms were all white with flour and her apron was stained so she gave me a penny and told me to run down as fast as I could.

Well, the sugar cost three farthings and the shopman said he didn't have any farthings and would I take sweets instead. I said yes but when I got home my mother said, 'Where's the farthing?' I told her what had happened and she said, 'Take the sweets back and get matches'.

After I got home again my mother gave me a telling off for being so silly as to believe the shopman. She said that he was only trying to get me to spend more on old rubbish and I should be smarter than a man with a wee huckster of a shop.

I know she is right but next time I have some money I will still buy Riley's toffee rolls from him. You get twelve for a ha'penny but he always throws in an extra one.

Sunday 28th April 1912

It was dry today but not very warm. In the afternoon we all went upstairs on the open-topped tramcar to Castle Junction which Father says is the centre of the tramway system. We walked along Donegall Place where all the fashionable shops are. Mother says she could never afford to shop in the likes of Anderson and McAuley's but she looked in all the windows just the same. Tommy and I were more interested in the large bell in an open frame which hangs above the clock. The building is so tall that Father took us to the other side of the road so that we could see it properly. Then Mother looked in the windows of Robinson and Cleaver's which she says has electric light and an elevator just like they have in America. On the front of the building there are carvings of famous customers and I recognised one as Queen Victoria. Next to Robinson and Cleaver's there is a really huge building which Father says is the largest linen warehouse in Belfast. I looked up and counted twelve big windows across and six windows high.

We crossed the road and went into the grounds of the grandest building in Belfast, the new City Hall. It is six years old and is the most wonderful building I have ever seen. Father carried Eileen all the way round and then Mother opened her bag and brought out the leftover scones from the visitors. It was like having a picnic outside a palace.

Monday 29th April 1912

Mother kept Mary off school today because she felt ill and my mother was afraid she had got a chill from being out so long yesterday. Ever since Mary was in hospital last year Mother worries if she so much as sneezes.

Tommy and I had watched as the nurse carried Mary out to the big dark green coloured ambulance which took her to the fever hospital at Purdysburn. She had diptheria and they kept her in hospital for six weeks.

I went with Father to bring her home because Mother had to stay in the house with Tommy and Eileen. We walked all the way from the tramcar terminus to Purdysburn and I can still remember the awful smell in the hospital there. When we came out Father had to get a wee pony and trap to bring the three of us back down to the tramline. Then we got on the tramcar and came home. Everybody fussed over Mary for ages. They must have thought she was never going to get out of Purdysburn.

Mary was still in Mother's bed when we came home from school today and Mother had lit a fire in the bedroom to keep her warm. Tommy played his mouthorgan to try to cheer her up and I gave her one of my best marlies. Mother coaxed her to take some hot marrowbone soup and she fell asleep afterwards. She looks very small lying there with her head in the middle of the big bolster.

A plan of my house

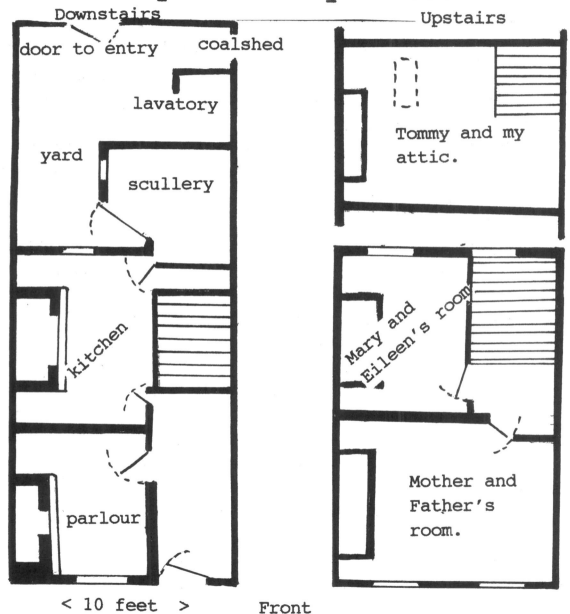

Downstairs

door to entry coalshed

lavatory

yard

scullery

kitchen

parlour

Upstairs

Tommy and my attic.

Mary and Eileen's room

Mother and Father's room.

< 10 feet > Front

Tuesday 30th April 1912

It was my turn to empty the po this morning and when I came back inside Mary was sitting up in bed and looking for her breakfast. Mother came up and said she was a good lot better but she would keep her in bed to be on the safe side. My mother was starting her spring cleaning so she wasn't going out anyway.

There is a lot to clean in our house. Tommy and I sleep up in the attic and there are two bedrooms below us, my mother and father sleep in one and Mary and Eileen are in the other. Downstairs we have our parlour, our kitchen and the scullery. Our lavatory is outside next to the coalshed in the yard which my mother says is badly in need of whitewashing.

I got all my sums right in school and Mr.Cunningham used them to mark all the others. I like Mr.Cunningham and I showed him my Titanic scrapbook. He said it had been such a tragedy and I should never forget what man's greed could lead to. I asked my father what he meant but he said Mr.Cunningham was speaking in riddles.

After tea Bertie and Hugh called for Tommy and me and we played churchie in the street. The breadcart came past on its way back to the bakery and Hugh bought four buns for us. His father had given him a penny when he had a lot of drink taken because his dog won a rosette at the show. It's not such a bad old dog after all!

My
Titanic
Scrapbook

by

James McDermott
Belfast, Ireland, April 1912

LAUNCH OF THE TITANIC

Impressive Spectacle at the Queen's Island

In the presence of thousands of spectators, the S.S. Titanic, which will share with the Olympic the distinction of being one of the two largest vessels afloat, was launched from Messrs. Harland and Wolff's yard at the Queen's Island yesterday.

The clanging of the hammers was heard all over the ship as the preparations for the launch were developed, but the men using them were for the most part hidden from view. On the deck the figures of the workers whose duty it was to see to the drag ropes and cables were dwarfed and blurred by the distance which separated them from the people down below.

The ceremony had been fixed for a quarter past twelve, and ten minutes before that time a red flag was hoisted at the stern of the vessel. Five minutes later two rockets were discharged, and shortly afterwards the explosion of another rocket was heard, and at 12.13 the spectators had the joy and satisfaction of seeing the vessel in motion. It was a wonderful and awe-inspiring sight, and a thrill passed through the crowd as their hopes and expectations were realised. The ship glided down to the river with a grace and dignity which for the moment gave one the impression that she was conscious of her own strength and beauty, and there was a roar of cheers as the timbers by which she had been supported yielded to the pressure put upon them. She took to the water as if she were eager for the baptism, and in the short space of 62 seconds she was entirely free.

BELFAST NEWSLETTER
1st June 1911

DEPARTURE OF THE TITANIC
The World's Largest Vessel

The new Royal Mail triple-screw steamer Titanic, which has been built by Harland & Wolff Ltd. for the White Star Line, left the deepwater wharf shortly after ten o'clock yesterday morning for Southampton, whence she will sail on her maiden voyage to New York on 10th inst. The usual scenes of bustle and animation attending the departure of a great liner were witnessed from an early hour in the morning, and as the hawsers were cast off, the Titanic - the largest vessel in the world - floated proudly on the water, a monument to the enterprise of her owners and ingenuity and skill of the eminent firm who built her.

She was at once taken in tow by the powerful tugs which were in attendance and the crowds of spectators who had assembled on both sides of the river raised hearty cheers as she was towed into the channel. The mammoth vessel presented an impressive and picturesque spectacle, looking perfect from keel to truck, while the weather conditions were happily of a favourable character.

BELFAST NEWSLETTER
3rd April 1912

When the tugs were left behind the compasses were adjusted, after which a satisfactory speed run took place, and the latest triumph of the shipbuilder's art then left for Southampton, carrying with her the best wishes of the citizens of Belfast.

ICEBERG 70 MILES IN LENGTH

THE TITANIC SINKING
NO DANGER OF LOSS OF LIFE

The new White Star liner Titanic which was built in Belfast and was delivered to her new owners less than a fortnight ago, has been in a collison with an iceberg off the coast of Newfoundland, and latest accounts report that she is sinking.

The disaster is reported to have occurred about 10.30 on Sunday night and wireless messages were flashed out for assistance. These were picked up by the Virginian of the Allan Line, about 200 miles distant, and she at once responded to the call for aid.

The operator of the Virginian kept up constant communication, but suddenly the communication stopped. Meanwhile the sister ship of the Titanic, the Olympic and also the White Star liner the Baltic took up the messages for help, and at once proceeded with all speed to the rescue.

Great excitement prevailed in Belfast, from which city many of the working crew came, and at the various shipping offices there were many anxious inquiries.

BELFAST TELEGRAPH 15th APRIL 1912

RECEPTION OF THE NEWS IN BELFAST

General Feeling of Regret

LOCAL PASSENGERS AND SAILORS ON BOARD

Nowhere has the news of the mishap to the Titanic been received with more sincere regret than in Belfast - the birthplace of the huge vessel- and fuller details concerning the accident are eagerly awaited. Like all the fleet of the White Star Line, she was built by Messrs.Harland & Wolff,Ltd., at the Queen's Island Shipbuilding Works, and the construction of the world's biggest ship, like that of her immediate predecessor and sister ship, the Olympic, was followed with the keenest interest by the community generally. It will be remembered that she was launched on Wednesday, the 31st May, 1911, and the ceremony was witnessed by many thousands of spectators, including several who had come across the channel to be present at the scene, which was certainly an impressive one. It may be said that she represents the very latest ideas, not only in regard to construction,but also in the matter of equipment, and that she cost close to two millions sterling. There was no public inspection prior to her departure from Belfast, but those who were specially privileged to make a tour through the great ship after her completion were deeply impressed by the immense size of the Titanic as well as by the general excellence of her accommodation - special attention being attracted by the magnificent suite of rooms for millionaires and other wealthy passengers. The Titanic left Belfast on the morning of Tuesday, the 2nd inst.,just a fortnight ago today, and proceeded to Southampton to take her place in the Atlantic service. On her departure she was accompanied by the best wished of the citizens, and none of those who watched her slowly gliding down the harbour and the lough anticipated that the voyage would have such a disastrous ending. Her sailing from Belfast had been delayed for a day by the tempestuous weather and the heavy seas prevailing, but the conditions on the morning of her actual departure were highly favourable,and, like the Olympic, she steamed away amid brilliant sunshine.

Amongst those on board the ill-fated liner at the time of the disaster was Mr. Thomas Andrews, jun., one of the directors of Messrs. Harland & Wolff Limited. It is highly probable that Lord Pirrie,K.P., chairman of the firm, would, in accordance with his usual custom, have been on board, as the representative of the builders, had it not been for the serious illness which confined him to his bed, but from which he is now recovering.

BELFAST NEWSLETTER
16th April 1912

1,455 PASSENGERS ON BOARD

A Few of Those on the Titanic Worth £50,000,000

The number of passengers on board the Titanic when she left Queenstown on her voyage, including the Cherbourg passengers, was, says Reuter:-

First Class	350
Second Class	305
Third Class	800
Crew	903
Total	2,358

The total mail on board was 3,418 sacks. At Cherbourg 142 first-class, thirty second-class and about eighty third-class passengers were embarked.

Many of the first-class passengers were well-known American multi-millionaires who were returning to the States after a holiday stay in this country.

"At a moderate estimate," a prominent American resident in London told *The Daily Mirror* yesterday, "the passengers represent a wealth of at least £50,000,000. Two of them alone are worth £20,000,000!"

Forthwith this gentleman compiled the following table showing the wealth of a few of the passengers:-

Colonel J.J.Astor	-	£10,000,000
Mr.G.D.Widener	-	10,000,000
Mr.Isodor Straus	-	4,000,000
Mr.B.Guggenheim	-	2,000,000
Mr.C.M.Hays	-	1,500,000
Mr.Wm.Dulles	-	1,000,000
Mr.Emil Taussig	-	1,000,000

THE DAILY MIRROR
16th April 1912

UNLUCKY CAPTAIN
Titanic's Commander in Command of Olympic at Time of Collision.

In command of the Titanic on her disastrous maiden voyage is Captain Edward John Smith, who has been a commander on the White Star Line for five-and- twenty years.

It is an unhappy coincidence that Captain Smith was in command of the Olympic last September on the occasion of her collision in the Solent with the cruiser Hawke.

In his evidence before the Admiralty Court he stated that he took charge of the Olympic on her first voyage last June, having formerly commanded the same company's liner Adriatic.

At the time of the collision the Olympic was in charge of a duly-licensed Trinity House pilot, and the judgment of the Court was that the collision was due to the Olympic's pilot.

Captain Smith, a Staffordshire man, born sixty years ago, is one of the best known and most popular shipmasters on the North Atlantic route.

Twice within eight months the two most colossal vessels that the world has ever seen have met with disaster. It is as though Nature grudged man his triumph over the nation-sundering ocean and revenged herself upon his tiny puny presumption..

Last year it was the Olympic whose mass of 45,000 tons collided with a warship that clave a hole in her side.

Yesterday it was the Titanic, mightier still in weight, yet for all her mammoth proportions a mere tub in the face of the overwhelming ice-mountain of the Atlantic.

So disaster crushed upon her, threatening 3,000 lives and the destruction in one blow of a floating township valued in gold at over two and a quarter millions.

But the inventions of man proved mightier than the brute force of the inanimate elements. The unsinkable ship builded by all the resources of centuries of science withstood the shock, messages carried by the harnessed waves of the air brought speedy help, and every life, it seems, was saved, and the ship herself proceeded unaided to port.

TWO GREATEST LINERS' PERIL

THE DAILY MIRROR 16th April 1912

THE TITANIC SUNK

COLLISION WITH ICEBERG

1,500 LIVES LOST

WIRELESS CALLS FOR HELP

LINERS TO THE RESCUE

The maiden voyage of the new White Star liner Titanic ended in disaster yesterday morning, the giant vessel sinking, with about 1500 of those on board, off the coast of Newfoundland, after collision with an iceberg.

The news of the collision was received on the night of the 14th inst. in Montreal by wireless telegraphy and several Atlantic liners also picked up the Titanic's messages calling for immediate assistance

The Virginian, Parisian, Baltic, Olympic and other vessels proceeded at full speed to the damaged liner, and over 600 of the passengers were subsequently transferred without mishap. It is officially stated that many lives have been lost.

The passengers are being conveyed to Halifax, Nova Scotia, where they are due to arrive tomorrow, and preparations are being made for their conveyance to New York.

BELFAST NEWSLETTER 16th APRIL 1912

THE NEW YORK TIMES

NEW YORK, TUESDAY, APRIL 16, 1912

TITANIC SINKS FOUR HOURS AFTER HITTING ICEBERG; 866 RESCUED BY CARPATHIA, PROBABLY 1250 PERISH; ISMAY SAFE, MRS. ASTOR MAYBE, NOTED NAMES MISSING

Col.Astor and Bride Isador Straus and Wife and Maj.Butt Aboard

"RULE OF SEA" FOLLOWED

Women and Children Put Over in Lifeboats and Are Supposed to be Safe in Carpathia

FRANKLIN HOPEFUL ALL DAY

Manager of the Line Insisted Titanic Was Unsinkable Even After She Had Gone Down

J.Bruce Ismay Making First Trip on Gigantic Ship That Was to Surpass All Others.

PARTIAL LIST OF THE SAVED.

Includes Bruce Ismay, Mrs. Widener, Mrs. H. B. Harris, and an Incomplete name, suggesting Mrs. Astor's.

Special to The New York Times.

CAPE RACE, N. F.; Tuesday, April 16.—Following is a partial list of survivors among the first-class passengers of the Titanic, received by the Marconi wireless station this morning from the Carpathia, via the steamship Olympic:

Mrs. JACOB P. —— and maid.
Mr. HARRY ANDERSON.
Mrs. ED. W. APPLETON.
Mrs. ROSE ABBOTT.
Miss G. M. BURNS.
Miss D. D. CASSEBERE.
Mrs. WM. M. CLARKE.
Mrs. B. CHIBINACE.
Miss E. G. CROSSBIE.
Miss H. ROSEBIE.
Miss JEAN HIPACK.
Mrs. HY. B. HARRIS.
Mrs. ALEX. HALVERSON.
Miss MARGARET BAYS.
Mr. BRUCE ISMAY.
Mr. and Mrs. ED. KIMBERLEY.
Mr. F. A. KENNYMAN.
Miss EMILE KENCHEN.
Mr. G. F. LONGLEY.
Mrs. A. F. LEADER.
Miss BERTHA LAVORY.
Mrs. ERNEST LIVES.
Miss MARY CLINES.
Mrs. SINGRID LINDSTROM.
Mr. GUSTAVE J. LESNEUR.
Miss GIORGETTA A. MADILL.
Mme. MELICARD.
Mrs. TUCKER and maid.
Mrs. J. B. THAYER.
Mr. J. B. THAYER, Jr.
Mr. HENRY WOOLMER.
Miss ANNA WARD.
Mr. RICHARD M. WILLIAMS.
Mrs. F. M. WARNER.
Miss HELEN A. WILSON.
Miss WILLARD.
Miss MARY WICKS.
Mrs. GEO. D. WIDENER and maid.
Mrs. J. STEWART WHITE.
Miss MARIE YOUNG.
Mrs. THOMAS POTTER, Jr.
Mrs. EDNA S. ROBERTS.
Countess of ROTHES.

Mr. C. ROLMANE.
Mrs. SUSAN P. ROGERSON. (Probably Ryerson).
Miss EMILY B. ROGERSON.
Mrs. ARTHUR ROGERSON.
Master ALLISON and nurse.
Miss K. T. ANDREWS.
Miss NINETTE PANHART.
Miss E. W. ALLEN.
Mr. and Mrs. D. BISHOP.
Mr. H. BLANK.
Miss A. BASSINA.
Mrs. JAMES BAXTER.
Mr. GEORGE A. BAYT***
Miss C. BONNELL.
Mrs. J. M. BROWN.
Miss G. C. BOWEN.
Mr. and Mrs. R. L. BECKW***.
Miss RUTH TAUSSIG.
Miss ELLA THOR.
Mr. and Mrs. E. Z. TAYLOR.
GILBERT M. TUCKER.
Mr. J. B. THAYER.
Mr. JOHN B. ROGERSON.
Mrs. M. ROTHSCHILD.
Miss MADELEINE NEWELL.
Mrs. MARJORIE NEWELL.
HELEN W. NEWSOM.
Mr. FIENNAD OMOND.
Mr. E. C. OSTBY.
Miss HELEN R. OSTBY.
Mrs. MAMAM J. RENAGO.
Mlle. OLIVIA.
Mrs. D. W. MERVIN.
Mr. PHILIP EMOCK.
Mr. JAMES GOOGHT.
Miss RUBERTA MAIMY.
Mr. PIERRE MARECHAL.
Mrs. W. E. MINEHAN.
Miss APPIE RANELT.
Major ARTUR PEUCHEN.
Mrs. KARL H. BEHR.
Miss DESSETTE.

Mrs. WILLIAM BUCKNELL.
Mrs. O. H. BARKWORTH.
Mrs. H. B. STEFFASON.
Mrs. ELSIE BOWERMAN.

The Marconi station reports that it missed the word after "Mrs. Jacob P." In a list received by the Associated Press this morning this name appeared well down, but in THE TIMES list it is first, suggesting that the name of Mrs. John Jacob Astor is intended. This supposition is strengthened by the fact that, except for Mrs. H. J. Allison, Mrs. Astor is the only lady in the "A" column of the ship's pasenger list attended by a maid.

NAMES PICKED UP AT BOSTON.

BOSTON, April 15.—Among the names of survivors of the Titanic picked up by wireless from the steamer Carpathia here to-night were the following:

Mr. and Mrs. L. HENRY.
Mrs. W. A. HOOPER.
Mr. MILE.
Mr. J. FLYNN.
Miss ALICE FORTUNE.
Mrs. ROBERT DOUGLAS.
Miss HILDA SLAYTER.
Mrs. P. SMITH.
Mrs. BRAHAM.
Miss LUCILLE CARTER.
Mr. WILLIAM CARTER.
Miss CUMMINGS.
Mrs. FLORENCE MARE.
Miss ALICE PHILLIPS.
Mrs. PAULA MUNGE.
Mrs. JANE ——
Miss PHYLLIS O. ——
HOWARD B. CASE.
Miss MINEHAN.
Miss BERTHA ——

The Carpathia rescued the survivors from the lifeboats. The New York Times gives some of them.

Titanic Sinks – Many Perish – Disastrous End To Maiden Voyage

A REUTER'S cable, dated New York, Monday, 3.45a.m., says - A telegram from Cape Race at 10.25 on Sunday evening stated - The Titanic has struck an iceberg. The steamer said that immediate assistance was required.

Half and hour afterwards, another message was received saying that the Titanic was sinking by the head, and that the women were being taken off in lifeboats.

The liner Baltic also reported herself within 200 miles of the Titanic and says that she is speeding to help her. The last signals from the Titanic arrived at New York at 12.27 yesterday morning. The Virginian's operator says that these were blurred and ended abruptly.

The Titanic is under the command of Commander J. Smith who had been transferred from the Olympic. Among the passengers on board are Colonel and Mrs.J.J.Astor, Major A.W.Butt, President Taft's aide-de-camp; Mr.B.Guggenheim of the well-known banking family; Mr.C.M.Hays, president of the Grand Trunk Railway; Mr.Ismay of the White Star Line; the Countess of Rothes, Mr.W.T.Stead, Mr.Clarance Moore, and Mr.Isadore Straus.

There are 318 first class passengers on board.

IRISH NEWS   17th APRIL 1912

BELFAST FEELING
GLOOM IN THE CITY
OF THE LEVIATHAN'S BIRTH

In a special and grevious manner did yesterday morning's terrible tidings of the Titanic's foundering in the waste of ice-strewn water off the coast of Newfoundland strike home to the consciousness of the community in Belfast. It is not too much to say that every citizen experienced the sensation of reflected glory when the Titanic took her place amongst the great ocean going leviathans, and felt a certain satisfaction in being at all associated with the city which witnessed the production of the world's largest vessel. How the sentiment of civic pride was aroused by this triumph of talent and toil so auspiciously launched from the Queen's Island.

Remembering this it is very easy to understand that a very real feeling of public sorrow was created in Belfast by the series of Marconigrams in yesterday morning's newspapers which set forth bluntly and coldly story of the Titanic.

IRISH NEWS   18th APRIL 1912

BELFAST
NEWSLETTER
22nd April 1912

A New Titanic as beautiful and stately as the ship which now lies at the bottom of the Atlantic can be built. The industry and resources of Belfast are equal to such a task as that; but none of the precious lives which have been lost can ever be restored or adequately compensated for.

It is this feeling of irreparable loss which has caused a gloom to settle over the great shipbuilding yard in which the Titanic had her birth and neither time nor achievement can dispel the memory of the catastrophe or heal the grief that has taken possession of the hearts of men.